The Portrait

Of Victoria

Books by Brenda Rogers

The Damage Of Deception 4 - Book Series

Book one "The Damage of Deception"

Book Two "Empty Vows"

Book Three An Unknown Love"

Book Four A Promise Broken"

"Olivia's Cry"

Secret Tears

To Love, Cherish and Abuse"

As I sat on my dingy couch watching my little black and white television, I could feel myself falling right back into that depression. Doctor Adams's words once again soared through my mind.

"Ellen, you have a depressive disorder, and that is understandable after what you have been through. This is not uncommon, the feelings you have, the hurt you have locked deep inside, let me help you." you can turn this around; you can heal yourself, by letting go."

He had no clue what I was feeling, and it was easy for him to tell me to let it go, I would never let it go, how could I?

When the very reason for living, was taken from

me, my world and my life, and then I was tossed aside to deal with it.

So how can Doctor Adams just tell me to let it go and to get on with my life.

My life ended that night three years ago.

Chapter One

I grew up in a loving home, with parents that loved each other and displayed their affection. I had a brother and sister, both older than me, we weren't the average siblings, we didn't fight we did have our disagreements, but nothing that wasn't worked out before bedtime.

We loved each other and were best friends.

There were always huge gatherings at our house on Thanksgiving and Christmas with grandparents on my Dad's side, and Aunts and Uncles and many cousins; I thought I had the perfect family.

My childhood was a happy one.

I made good grades in school, my parents told me often how proud they were of me.

They had high hopes for all three of their children.

My life was so perfect that I didn't know how to handle the real life when hardship and heartache was present.

When I didn't have my mother and father or my siblings to run home to.

As a little girl sharing a room with my older sister I would tell her about my dreams of one day going to Paris, and being one of the beautiful lady I would see in photos or in the many magazines I had collected.

While kids my age were spending their allowance on toys or games, I was buying magazines about Paris, I had many posters of Paris on my side off the room.

My sister was always making fun of me.

"Ellen, you need to get your head out of the clouds, you are not ever going to Paris, why don't you dream like other kids your age and dream about Disney or something more realistic, more practical."

But I held on to my dream growing up and talked about it often, even when I knew my family were getting sick of hearing about Paris., they would just humor me, but one day I would show them all.

Chapter Two

Beginning in Junior high school I was head cheer leader and I continued to hold that title through my high my school years,.

I was very popular in school just like my older brother and Sister were.

In high school, I got a part time job, even thought my parents had always supported my dreams, they told me I had to finance my Paris dream on my own, just like they had to finance their dream of me going to college, so I worked hard all through high school saving for my trip to Paris, missing out on a lot of things, but I knew one day Paris would be worth it.

Patty and Angie, my two best friend since grade school and I, would spend two glorious months there, before we headed off to college, and became responsible Adults.

I enjoyed my school years and I looked forward to college, I would miss the carefree days of high school, the proms, and the games.

I dated Jeremy, the Captain of the football *team all through high school, we were an idol, voted to be the most likely to succeed as a couple, but when high school was over, so was our romance, we didn't share the same feelings as so many thought we had, outside off school and all that applies with high school, we had nothing more in common, and we parted as friends.*

I had my eye on someone else, someone that took my breath away, every time he looked at me, something Jeremy was never able to do.

He was my brother's supervisors at his work.

I had met him a few times and he was nothing like the boys in high school.

He was charming and very good looking, he was very courteous, and I was attracted to him the first time Don introduced me to him at their company picnic.

When I pulled in our driveway, my brother was washing his car, so I thought this would be a great opportunity to talk to him about sitting me up with Matt.

"Hey Don, what are you doing?" "What does it look like I'm doing?" Ignoring his sarcastically tone.

"Brother, I want you to do something for me," I said in my sweetest voice.

"I'm not washing your car; I don't have time I'm picking Char up in a few hours."

"That's not what I was going to ask you, even though my car could use a good cleaning."

"Don, you should set me up with Matt."

"Matt? My boss?"

" Yeah, Matt your boss"

"No way!" he rolled his eyes at me.

"Come on Don, I think he is so cute and I want

to go out with him." "No sis, I'll wash your car instead." " You said he didn't have a girlfriend," "That's right and I'm pretty sure if he wanted one, he could get one on his own, he doesn't need my help.

"But Don, I need your help, so give me one good reason why you can't talk to him about me?"

" Because we're not in high school anymore, find your own date, and besides what about Jeremy?" I thought you two were an item."

"No we broke up, we are just friends now"

"I knew you two were not meant for each other."

"Come on Don, just ask Matt about me, find out if he likes me"

"Okay, I'll pass him a note in gym class tomorrow." He joked. there was his sarcastically tone again, I hated begging my

brother, but I wanted to get to know Matt and I knew Don was my answer, since he worked with him every day."

"So you're saying, you won't help me?"

"Ellen I can't ask my boss to go out with my younger sister, he would think I was nuts." " Okay fine! But let me bring back something to your memory, do you recall a little episode involving you and a little redhead that your girlfriend knew nothing about and I covered for you, because you convinced me it was all innocent on your part?"

"Oh, so you are going to blackmail me?" He sounded shocked. "Hey whatever it takes big brother,"

"Fine I will talk to him, but I'm not making any promises, so don't hold your breath!"

"Thank you" I waved to him over my shoulder as I walked inside the house.

I was saving that little piece of dirt on my brother, even if I did know nothing really happened with him and the red head, his fiancé Char might not understand.
The truth was I would have nerve told Char anything, but I'm glad Don didn't know that.
I should have made him wash my car also.
I passed the window and seen Don talking in his phone, and I hoped he was talking to Matt, it didn't take long to find out while I was still watching, he got off of his phone and was headed inside house and yelled my name.

"Yeah" You have a date tonight with Matt." " Are you serious?" " Yes we are meeting him at Angelo's in two hours." " Two hours? "Yup."

"Oh my goodness, I immediately went into panic mode, two hours to shower, wash and fix my hair and find something amazing to wear. An hour later Don knocked on my door, to find me with a bed full of clothes and my hair up in a towel. "What is the big deal? it is just dinner and a movie, not the prom."

I tried to act grown up and not be nervous .
I sat in the off Don's car while he went inside to get Char, his fiancé.
I kept telling myself it was just a date and I was doing pretty good, until Char got into the car.
"Oh my goodness, you're going out with Matt? He is so cute!" " Hey, what am I? Chopped liver?" Don said.. "You are cute too, honey" Char patted his back. "Well I was trying not to be nervous, thanks a lot Char"

"Oh it will be fine, he's just a guy, a very good looking guy, but still just a guy," she laughed.

Chapter Three

Once at the restaurant the guys did most of the talking and it was mostly about work, but I didn't mind just being close to Matt was all that mattered, no matter where the conversation went.

When we were leaving the restaurant, Matt pointed toward his car, "I'm parked over there, {all I could think was I get to ride with Matt}

He was real easy to talk to, and just the short ride to the theater we discovered we had a lot in common.

Sitting so close to him in the movie theater made my heart flutter and I had sweaty palms, I hoped he didn't try to hold my hand...

Walking out of the theater, the four of us lingered and talked, I didn't want to say good night.

"Ellen, can I give you a ride home?" "Okay, thanks,"

He put his hand in the small of my back as we walked to his car. We talked about his job and Don, he told me he really liked my brother and he was glad he set us up, because he also noticed me the first time he saw me.

At my house he got out and opened my car door than he walked me to my door.

"Do you like to play miniature golf?" "I love

miniature golf." I said a little too hasty.

He laughed. "Would you like to go tomorrow evening?" "Sure" I said. "Okay, I will pick you up around five" "Okay, see you tomorrow".

I love miniature golf? Why did I say that, I'm not sure I even like Miniature golf, but I am sure I like Matt and would have agreed to go anywhere he suggested? I haven't played miniature golf enough times to determine if I do or don't love it, I hope he didn't think that I sounded stupid.

The next evening after playing two games I can now determine that I do in fact love playing miniature golf, not real sure if it was playing golf or being with Matt for those four hours, but I had the time of my life, we played two games, and would have went for a third, but the place was closing.

Matt walked me to the door than kissed me goodnight.

"So you and Matt getting kind of chummy aren't you?" Don said when I walked inside the house. "Why do you say that?" "I saw you two kiss" He smiled. "It was one kiss." I dreamily said. "What were you doing spying on me?" "No I heard a car and looked out the window. He said with a snicker.....

Matt and I spent every free minute we could together he became a part of the family.

Matt and I were invited to his parent's house for supper, over the months I had come to the realization that his mother did not like me much, but I felt like she was giving me a chance or she was trying to please her son.

Matt had told me, because he was an only child, she was very protective of him and had never thought any girl was good enough.

It was a quiet and stressful evening and I was glad when it came time for us to leave.

Matt's Dad was a man of few words so I didn't know how he felt about Matt dating me.

Chapter Four

Hey Ellen, family meeting," Don said when I walked in the front door.

"Okay, hold on for a sec." "Ellen, now" My Dad appeared in the doorway,

I knew something was wrong by his tone of voice. In the living room my sister Sara was sitting in the chair, it appeared like she had been crying but lately with her it was hard to tell, she was always sad. Mom was lying on the couch with pillows behind her head, my sister Sara was three years older than me, and we used to be so close until she married a guy that my parents didn't approve of, and they were right, he was a loser, he didn't work most of the time, she had two kids and held down a full time job, the house they lived in was junky, but she wouldn't listen to our parents, they tried to get her to go to college and make something of her life, but she decided it was her life and now she regretted it, she hardly ever smiled anymore and her husband controlled everything she did,, my parents could only see their grandchildren when he allowed it.

I felt so sorry for her and I missed that fun loving sister that I had shared a room with growing up, but she was long gone.

I knew Mom hadn't been feeling good lately but

she said it was nothing, but this didn't look like nothing any more, the looks on my family's face said this was something and I wasn't sure I was ready to find out what.

"Kid's I wanted to have this meeting to let you know your mother is sicker than what we thought, as you know she has been seeing a cardiology and he recommended for her too see a cardiac surgeon, and we did, and the Doctor has said your mother needs to have open-heart surgery."

"What did they find wrong with her heart?" I asked. All of a sudden fear gripped my own heart at just the word open-heart surgery.

"Is that why she has been taking blood thinners?' Don asked. I didn't even know that she was. "So is it serious?" Sara wanted to know. "I'm afraid so, this procedure is difficult and there is risk involved.

No one spoke. "Hey, I'm sitting right here so please stop talking about me like I wasn't, and please know I'm not scared at all,, Doctor Willis comes highly recommended, and I will be just fine, so don't go worrying about me, I promise before long I will be back on my feet bossing everyone around just like old times."

I went and gave her a hug, "I know you will; besides you are too hateful to die." "That's right." She laughed. "So when will you have the surgery?" Sara came and joined us on the couch. The surgery will be at six am this Friday. Mom said. "That soon?" Don now sounded worried. "Hey the sooner I get it done, the sooner I can get better Son, besides I have to recover fast for you and Char's wedding " "Yes you do, because you will be my favorited girl there." he said as he kissed her on the cheek.

After our parents went to bed for the night it gave me a chance to spend some time with Sara,

I couldn't believe she had stayed as long as she had usually she a curfew ordered by her husband.

I talked about me and Matt, and I told her that I was in love with him. “Ellen, please go slowly, don't mess your life up like I did, because you will regret it”

Sara had such a sad tone about her voice now; there was no joy as before. “We are taking it slow he knows I will be going to college once I get back from Paris.” “Oh Paris, you have talked about Paris since you were a little girl and now just to think it's coming true for you, you are so lucky, I'm glad you didn't give up on your dream.”

“Hey I remember when you a dream, you talked about going to medical school and becoming a Doctor, what happened Sis? Why did you throw

all of your dreams away like that and break our parent's hearts?"   "Because I was crazy, and I got pregnant with Kendall, and I thought Scott was different than what he turned out to be, I also thought having a baby I had no other choice but to get married. Because I thought that would break our parent's heart"

Chapter Five

Matt stayed at the hospital with me, which I was grateful, it helped to ease my nerves, the Doctor was very positive about the surgery and he took time to talk to all of us and to let us know what to expect after the surgery.

He said the procedure should take anywhere from three to six hours.

It was the longest day of all of our lives. We were

all relieved when he came out and told us that the surgery went well. Mom would be in the hospital for at least ten days.

We knew Dad wouldn't leave her side, even when we stayed with mother.

He would only go home just long enough time to shower and change his clothes.

We were all so glad when Mom got to come home we knew she was going to need a lot of care,

The doctor said it could take up to two months before she would start to feel better.

We took turns in her care, I hated to see her in so much pain,Dad was the main care giver.

His boss agreed to Dad's request when he had requested to do his job at home so he could be with her, I worried about him, he wasn't sleeping because mom couldn't sleep. He wasn't eating like he should, but he wouldn't listen to us, I tried to always be available to help just so he would take a break. We all knew it was hard on him to see the love of his life in so much discomfort.

Matt was at our house almost every day and I loved having him so near, he gave not just me but my family comfort.

He would talk to my mom and read to her, I could tell she enjoyed Matt's company and that made me glad.

As the weeks turned into months She was constantly in and out of the hospital, but nothing seem to be helping, she would have good days and then she would have very bad days. It was taking its toll on Dad, he worried all the time that he was going to lose her, but I wouldn't let myself think about that, even though I could see her health declining every day.

To make matters worse, she developed an infection; she was back in the hospital. As the weeks passed she just grew worst every day, I don't know all the reasons because Dad didn't want to worry us, but we knew something was terribly wrong.
One evening I had returned from a date with Matt, I had just started up to my room trying hard not to wake my parents when Dad appeared at the Mom's doorway

"Ellen, your mother and I need to have a talk with you." My Dad sounded so serious. "Should I call Don?" "No, this is not a family meeting; we just need to talk to you."" "I already knew. They were going to try to talk me into keeping my plans to go

to Paris.

Mom looked so thin and fragile lying in the hospital bed that Dad had got for her

"Honey, come sit with me," she said in her weak voice. I went and sat on the side of her bed...

"Ellen, there is no need to pretend like I'm going to get better." "But mom, we don't know that."

I fought to hold my tears, just like so many times before, but I hated it when she talked this way.

"No Ellen, I do know that, and that is why you I feel like it is time we tell you something even though your father doesn't feel it necessary, I feel it is an essential that you know."

I stopped her before she could continue. "Mom, if this is about my trip to Paris, I have already told both off you, I'm not going, and there is nothing more you can say to make me change my mind."

"No Ellen, it's not about your trip, but I want you

to listen to me please"

I could tell she was having a hard time talking and breathing, so I just listened. "Ellen, you have heard me talk about my baby sister Riley?" "Yes mom, you said you hadn't seen her since she was a teenager and they think she may have drowned." "That's corrected, but there is something we have never told you, but I want you know now." "Know what?" I asked, wondering why she was wasting her precious breath on this conversation. "Riley was the baby of the family, and she was spoiled. Our parents and even our two brothers gave her everything she wanted, because she was so petite and beautiful, and she used her beauty to get what she wanted, even with me.

After our parents were killed, Riley was only ten years old, so I finished raising her, and I'm now sorry to say I too gave her everything she wanted.

When she was sixteen she ran away with an older gentleman, because Riley hated being cooped up here, she had high hopes and unrealistic dreams, she always said she wanted to experience the finer things in life.

I begged her not to go, even your father tried to talk to her, but she wouldn't listen to either of us.

"When Don, your brother was four and Sara was two, Riley came back, I was so happy to have her back, but she hadn't come home for good, she came back because she was pregnant and she had decided to put the baby in foster care, but me and your father couldn't let happened, so we talked Riley into giving us her baby and she agreed, when you were born, at Ryley's request she never saw you, you were put into my arms.

I heard my own self gasp.

But Ellen you were in my heart from the day my

sister told me about you, and I couldn't have loved you more if I would have gave birth to you"

I couldn't believe what I was hearing, I looked over at Dad and he was crying, so I knew this was all true. "You are not my mother?" I let my tears freely fall. "Oh baby, I will always be your mother and you will always be my daughter." She began to cry and shake, Dad came over, and gave her a shot, and tried to comfort her because she was getting excited, and she began to cough which hurt her chest.

"Oh mom, it's okay, calm down, it's okay, I love you, I know you are my mother and I love you, please don't cry" I put my arms around her until she became still again. "Ellen, I'm sorry I didn't tell you before, but I couldn't stand the thought of you being hurt with knowing.

"Mom, now you listen to me okay, thank you for

telling me, but it doesn't change anything, I'm still me and I thank you for loving me enough to take me and to care and love me, and I don't want you to even think about it anymore, promise me"

"I promise, I love you Ellen" She whispered as she fell asleep from the shot my dad had gave to calm her down when she had become excited.

Once outside her room, I had lots of questions for my father, like what really happened to my mother. And who was my real father? Who did I look like? Had I ever seen pictures of my mom? I wanted to know everything, did Don and Sara know? "Donny knows, but Sara was too young, and we never told her." He said. I didn't know if I was sad or glad about that, I had so many mixed emotions going on in my head at that moment.

He took me up to the attic and a few minutes later he pulled out a photo album, he showed me pictures of mom and Riley, my grandparents, but he said they never knew who my father was. Mom was right Riley was beautiful.

"Honey as you can see you look just like your mom." "What happened to her?" I asked. "No one really knows for sure, your mother has spends many sleepless nights crying and worrying about her baby sister but still no real answers. After you were born, she went away again and we never saw her after that."

" But mom said something about they think she drown?"

"Years ago there was a rumor that she was seen on a liner that sunk, a lot of people were killed, and there were some people that were never found

and that includes Riley, so your mother has never had that closure.

My father held me as I cried, I had so many questions that couldn't be answered, I couldn't talk to Mom and get her upset anymore, and she was too weak.

We knew we wasn't going to have her much longer, my heart was so broken for so many reasons.

My mother, to me was the greatest woman in the world and every night I cried myself to sleep just wondering if I would see her the next day.

How can my heart take this in right now? Don and Sara was not even my brother and sister but my cousins, I wept just coming to that conclusion.

That night, I laid in bed. but my mind wouldn't turn off, I just couldn't comprehend that my whole life has been a lie, I wish she hadn't made the decision to tell me, why did they feel like I needed to know, why didn't Dad take into consideration that I had enough to handed just to think I may be losing my mom, and it was even harder to think of her as my Aunt. Now my deepest fears and anxieties are to come to the realization that people leave...even mothers go away.

I don't know why I was feeling grief over the loss of a relationship with a woman I never met, and the grief of losing the woman that I have called Mom all my life.

The next morning I knew I needed to get out of the house, I needed to see Matt.

After I showered and dressed, I quietly stepped in to Mom's room, Dad was sleeping in his lazy-boy chair, but mom was awake. "Good Morning," I said as I kissed her cheek. "Can I get you something, coffee or some breakfast?"

"Oh no dear, I'm sick at my stomach this morning, so I better not have anything right now, but thank you." "You are welcome, I'm meeting Matt, so I will be leaving now," "Okay, tell him I said hi, won't you" "Yes I will," I quietly left the room as not to wake Dad.

Chapter Six

It felt so good to be in Matt's arms, I felt safe, and for just a little while I could forget about all my troubles. He always knew when something had me upset and today wasn't any exception, I wasn't really in the mood to talk about what I had learned last night, I guess I thought if I didn't talk about it, it would just go away. But Matt insisted on me telling him what was wrong... After I had finished telling him everything my parents had told me, he held me while I cried. It seemed lately I was crying a lot on his shoulder.

"I just feel like I don't belong anywhere like I don't know who I am, I know that's sounds strange but It's how I feel, It seem to have changed everything about me, like I don't have a true family anymore, not real parents, or brother and sister, where do I fit in, where do I belong?" I cried.

"First of all you belong with me I want to be your family.

Ellen I know now isn't the time and I know here isn't the place, but I love you with all of my heart, Will you marry me?" At first it didn't sink in what he just ask me, I just looked at him, waiting for him to say something that just sounded like a marriage proposal, and when he only looked at me, waiting for an answer, I knew I didn't misunderstand him. "Matt, I will be leaving for college in just a few months." "I know, I'm not asking you to give up college, I will wait for you forever if that's what it takes." "Oh Matt, I will marry you, I love you and I can't stand the thought of being away from you for so long."

"It will pass quickly then we will have our whole lives to be together." He said.

More tears fell but they were happy tears.

Chapter Seven

SUnday's Matt spent with me and most of the day was spent in mom's room, he talked to her and read from the bible to her, Mom and Dad really liked Matt, they told me many times how happy they were for us, Mom had cried when we announced our engagement to her.

Dad just said "I'm happy for both of you but just remember four years is a long time"

Don's words were..... "I better get a raise for this."

Every moment of my time when I wasn't with Matt, I was with Mom, we never spoke anymore about what I was told because I didn't want her to be upset, even though I still had a lot of questions. I watched everyday as she got weaker and it broke my heart to know she wouldn't be at my wedding or when I finished college or when I have children, when she was sleeping I would think of these things. Don and Sara spend every weekend with her and our Dad never left her room for a long amount of time. He looked thin and older than what he was.

I had thought long and hard on my decision and I knew I would have people very upset with me, but I made my mind up and I knew the sooner I told everyone the better it would be for me,
I could get rid of the anxiety of telling them.

"Dad, can I talk to you for a moment, please, I didn't feel like there was a reason to upset my mother by her knowing. "Dad, I want to tell you that I will not be going to college." "Is this a joke?" He already sounded mad. "No, Dad, I have thought about this, and I cannot leave her."

"Ellen, this is your life, don't just toss it away."

"Dad, you won't leave her room for more than ten minutes, but you expect me to leave her for four years, when I leave here in two weeks, I will never see her again and you know it.

College can wait, but my mother can't" I began to cry he put his arms around me. "It's okay, I understand, and I can't blame you, I ask him not to tell mother and he promised me he wouldn't.

That night I told Matt.

"Ellen, this has nothing to do with us getting married does it, because I don't want you to regret our marriage later on." "No Matt, it is for the reasons I told you, I can't leave my mother."

After a few minutes he said...."I don't mean to sound selfish, but I didn't think I could live that long without you,"

"Will this put our marriage on hold?" "No Matt, I want to marry you as soon as I can."

"You can still go to college after we are married, you shouldn't give up on that dream, you could just go closer to home?"

"Yes when the time is right, I will."

Three days before I was to leave for college, we said goodbye to our mother, she passed away with all of her family at her bedside. I had never experienced this kind of pain, I was so thankful I had Matt to help me.

None of us left Dad alone, after the funeral, he wouldn't leave her room, his grief was so strong, I wondered if he was going to make it without her. As time passed very slowly, he began to let her go little by little, me and Sara were allowed to clean the room and take the hospital bed out and sell it, we decided to change everything about the room so when he would go in there he wouldn't have the constant bad memories of her suffering.

We painted and Don and Matt put a new floor down and we made the room into an office for our Dad. The upstairs bedroom was made into Dad's bedroom, we tried to change things for him, we knew he couldn't sleep in the bedroom mom had passed away in.

Everyone was busy with Don and Char's wedding preparations which was a good thing because it took our minds off of everything.

I knew that we all wanted our lives to go back to normal, but it was going to take time, changing a room was not going to change our broken hearts.

Chapter Eight

Matt and I went out to pick up pizza for super and when we returned Don was sitting in his car.

Matt took the pizza inside and I went up to his car.

"Hey, Pizza's here." I could tell right away, he was crying, and my heart went into a panic.

"Don, what is wrong?" "Char called off the wedding, she said she was in love with someone

else." I quickly got inside his car and put my arms around him, "Oh Don, I'm so sorry." I cried with him. "Can you believe it, two weeks before our wedding, she tells me she is in love with someone else." "How is that possible?" I asked.

"I will tell you, it's because she has been cheating on me for a while now, she told me she didn't want to tell me because of everything I was going through with losing mom, I wasted three years on her, how could she do this?"

"Don, I'm so sorry, please comes inside the house."

"No, I just need to be alone right now.'

" Is there anything I can do?"

"No, you go ahead, I will be okay, I will be in a little while."

My heart was broken for Don, I know how much he loved Char and I thought she loved him.

Matt and I were planning on waiting a year after Don was married before we had our wedding, but I was very used to my plans changing.

I told Matt what happened and he went out to talk to Don.

Gradually he started to get over his break-up with Char, or so it seemed, five months later he announced that he had joined the Army. As much as I would miss my brother, I felt like it was for the best. At least he would be so busy, he wouldn't have time to grief over Char anymore.

It was hard to believe in just over a year's time everyone's life had changed so drastically.

My dream of Paris and college and now my wedding was not what I had expected it to be, but of Couse my life was so different than what I had expected it to be.

Because of all of our circumstances, and the fact that Matt's mother was against us getting married, it was my idea that we postpone our wedding for another year until things settled down., Matt wasn't very happy about it, but a wedding was support to be a joyous time, but it seemed that no one was displaying any type of joy right now.

The one person I thought would understand was my sister, but I was wrong.

"Ellen, you need to stop putting your life on hold,

first you gave up your dream of going to Paris and then college and now your wedding? Matt is a great guy and you are very lucky, please listen to your sister and take my advice don't blow this one!"

"This is my life and besides you're not my sister, your my cousin!" "What?" she just looked at me, "You are so weird." She said.

"Never mind, I will see you later." I walked out before I said more than what I should..

Because it was summer and the place I worked was busy, I put in a lot of hours, so I didn't see Matt as much as before and I missed him and I missed Don.

Dad was starting to look and act better now that he was out of the house and back at his job.

I was happy that he had moved on with his life.

But I wasn't happy when one day I came home from work and he had a lady friend over, I thought this was way too soon; mom had only been gone for a year.

"Hey Ellen I thought you would be out with Matt tonight." He looked shocked when I walked in the front door.

"I want you to meet someone; I stood in front of a very attractive and sophisticated woman. "Pat, this is my daughter Ellen" Dad sounded nervous like he just got caught with his hand in the cookie jar. "It's nice to meet you Pat"

I didn't mean it, is a matter of fact, I wanted to tell her to get out of my mother's house.

"Nice to meet you Ellen" and I could tell she didn't mean it either.

"If you will excuse me, I do have to get ready for my date with Matt.

"Okay have a good time" I didn't even answer my Dad, I just went to my room to change thankful I would be leaving the house soon, I held the tears in and I had decided not to cry on Matt's shoulder over this but to just let it go.

Chapter Nine

Matt had always been my sounding board, but I didn't want to become a burden to him, so I started keeping a lot of things inside. But that all changed when only a month after meeting Pat, they announced they were getting married.

I was in complete shock. "Dad, you can't be serious, you don't even know this woman" I cried.

"Ellen, I will always love your mother, but she is gone and if I could I would bring her back but I

can't, and Ellen try to understand, I need Pat just like you need Matt, I get lonely being by myself and Pat is my friend, we talk, she has made me laugh again, before her, I thought my life was over without your mother." "I'm sorry Dad but I just can't stand the thought of Pat living in my mother's house." "Pat feels the same way that is why I'm selling this house." "What! your selling our house?" "Ellen you are not a child anymore, I did talk to Pat about waiting until you and Matt are married, but she wants to sell it right away."

"Oh and what Pat wants she gets?"

"Honey rather you like it or not, I am marrying Pat and I am selling the house, I had hoped you would be understanding." "Have you told Don and Sara yet?" " I have spoken to Sara, but not Don"

"So what did Sara say?" "Actually she said she was happy for me." "Yea, she would." "Maybe one day, you will be also." He said.

"Well I guess it don't really matter how I feel about it "; "In this matter, no it doesn't, I'm sorry Ellen"

So once again I became a burden to Matt. " I just can't understand how he can marry so soon after Mom? How can he just forget about her, so quickly?"

"Ellen, don't you think you are being kind of hard on your father, you know he loved your mom, the man never left her side for a moment, we watched as he worried and cared for her, he made his own self sick from it, and you know he will never forget her, but I agree with him, she is gone and not by his choice and she will never return, your dad is still a young man, do you really want him

to spend the rest of his life alone and being miserable?" "No, of course not, it just seems like my whole life has been changed, like a rug was pulled out from under me, first I found out the woman I love with all my heart is not even my real mother, then I lose her, my brother goes away and now my dad is getting married, and selling the only home I had ever known, when the house sells, I have nowhere to go."

"Yes you do, we can get married instead of putting it off, start a family with me Ellen, with the man that loves you more than anything."

Chapter Ten

That night instead of worrying about Dad's wedding, I was thinking about my own. I plan on asking Patty and Angie to be my bridesmaids and of course Sara to be my maid of honor, my niece Kendall to be my flower girl and my nephew Jason to be my ring bearer.

We both agreed on a small wedding because at this point we weren't sure if his family would even attend the ceremony.

I called Patty and Angie to see if we could have lunch together.

They were both very excited for me, unlike my sister.

"Are you share you are not rushing into this marriage because your losing your home and a place to live". "I don't understand you Sara, first you tell me I shouldn't postpone my marriage because I might lose Matt, now you are questioning why I'm getting married so soon?"

I'm just saying be sure that is all."

"Did you tell Dad to be sure? Or did you just give him your blessings?"

" Is this where your attitude is coming from because I gave Dad my blessings and why shouldn't I? He suffered right along with Mom's suffering; he was a loving and supportive husband, he has did nothing wrong he deserves a

little happiness now."

" You are right, I'm sorry, I guess I just have some issues I'm trying to work out" "You know I'm always here if you need to talk" she said.

"Thank you, but there is something I need you to help me with" "What's that?" "Dad wants us to pack things up in the house before it goes on the market and to give it a good cleaning, he said we can have what we want."

"I'll help you, how about tomorrow since I'm off work for a few days"

"That's fine."

"I will be there as soon as I drop the kids off at school"

I knew I had to work this whole issue out on my own about what my parents told me, I didn't realize just how much this was bothering me.

As I was packing things up in my room I thought about talking to Sara but then she would know and I wasn't sure I wanted her to know that we weren't really sisters.

After a few cups of coffee, the rest of the day

was spent with us looking through pictures albums and reminiscing.

"We had such an easy life growing up, I'm so thankful for our parents." "Yes so Am I, I wish I would have been more submissive to them when they told me not to get married and to go to college, I was very wrong in my decisions, I never once took into consideration how much I hurt them." She said.

"Sara what is in the past is in the past. It does no good to worry about it now" I turned another page in the album; it was pictures of one of our many family vacations. We laughed and we cried. There were photos Of Riley that would only mean something to me, I would take them later after Sara left. We didn't get a lot done, but I wasn't in a hurry to move out, Pat could wait.

Chapter Eleven

THree weeks later, the for sale sign was placed in our front yard, it was a sad site, I knew I had to accept the fact that my family no longer lived here.

But my mother's memories were in this house.

I knew that was why it was so hard for me to let it go.

I was happy that I was about to start my new life with Matt and to start my own familly and we both wanted lots of children.

It wasn't long after the house sold that Dad and Pat had their very expensive wedding and I wondered if this wedding was paid for from the sell of our home?' Sara asked me the same question.

None of his children were in his wedding but her two sons were, it didn't matter I didn't want to be in it anyway, I only came for my dad,

because believe me, I would much rather be at the dentist than here.

At the reception, we were totally ignored, when Dad did find the time to speak to us, Pat would rush him away to speak to someone else, and the looks she gave us were not nice.

There was a time Sara and I were standing alone talking, Pat came up to us and very sweetly said...."You know girls, you don't have to stay, this party could go on for hours and I know you both must be tired." She smiled and walked away.

We just looked at eachother., and decided she was right, we both were very tired of her.

When we found Dad and told him we were leaving his only reply was "Okay,"

After that I didn't hear much from my father, everytime I called his cell phone it went to his voice mail and he stopped returning my calls, when I called his home, she would always say he wasn't there and she would give him my message.

One time when I finaly got in touch with him I asked him if she ever gave him a messege from me? he said "No, but you have to understand, she is very busy."

I spent the next six months planning my wedding, I made up my mind that our wedding was going to be perfect, I was marrying the greatest man I ever knew and I loved him so much.
So I wanted everything to be just right, something we could cherish for the rest of our lives.
I was constantly planning and obsessing over the most smallest of details, yet somehow, I couldn't even remember my own name because I was so busy and I was so scared I was forgetting something, in the end I just wanted it to be over with, because I knew something was going to go wrong.
Matt kept telling me I was worrying too much, I knew he was right and I tried to stay calm and enjoy myself, after I made sure every I was dotted and every T was crossed.

Chapter Twelve

The morning of my wedding day in my bridal suite was nothing short of a three-ring circus. I was so preoccupied with trying to stay calm and just be in the moment that instead I had forgotten my bridal bouquet and my vail I had to send my sister which was also my hairdresser to get them for me, I just kept telling myself everything was going perfect, just a little set back, just because my hair and make- up wasn't done twenty minutes before I was to walk down the aisle in front of over a hundred people Everything was still okay.

As a young girl, I thought walking down the aisle on my wedding day was going to be the most incredible day of my life, but again I had always dreamed this day would take place in Paris.

I had never been so happy to see my maid of honor arrive.

Now my Make-up and hair could begin beautifying.

As I stood and looked in the mirror after she was all done, a tear escaped down my cheek, when I saw my sister's reflection in the mirror, I saw the same tear on her cheek, we made eye contact and smiled, we didn't have to speak because we both knew these tears was for our sweet mother.

My bridal bouquet happily made its way into my hand..

I was so graciously surprised when my brother walked into the room. "Don! I thought you said you couldn't make it?" " How could I miss my baby sister's Wedding?"

"Now I have my whole family here, I'm so happy,"

I gave him a hug.

Now my wedding day was perfect.

As we danced together for the first time as husband and wife Matt said something so sweet to me.

"Ellen I wish I could afford to take you to Paris for our honey moon, I love you so much I just want to build my world around you.

"Oh Matt, you are my Paris and it doesn't matter where I'm at, as long as you are there."

How could I be so lucky as to be marrying this great man.

That day I put away my girlish dreams, and exchanged them for reality.

"Honey, we are leaving now, Pat has a headache."

"But Dad, the reception has just started, we haven't did our father and daughter dance"

"I'm sorry Ellen, but she really wants to go."

"Then let her go, Don will take you home."

"I did suggest that, but she doesn't want me to stay

without her, I'm sorry." He hugged me goodbye. "Dad, do you even care that this is my wedding day and that you are breaking my heart?" "Ellen, what do you want me to do?, she is my wife." "I want you to stand up to her and tell her you are staying because it's your daughter's wedding day!"

I was getting very upset with my father.

"Well actually she knows the situation about your real mother, so she doesn't consider me your Dad."

"What?" I could not believe he just said that to me.

I was in total shock, I looked at him like I didn't even know him anymore.

"Do you feel that way now? Like you are not my real father?"

"Honey, I raised you and I love you, but we don't know who your father is, but it doesn't matter."

He reached to give me a hug again, but I stepped back and just turned and walked away.

I went into the lady's room and I cried.

I didn't understand why he would have said that to me, especially today.

"Ellen, Matt is looking everywhere for you"

My sister said when she came into the restroom looking for me.

"Why are you crying, what's wrong?"

"Nothing, I'm just upset with Dad right now."

"Why?" "because he said Pat wanted leave."

"Well just let her go, who cares if she leaves"

"I don't care if she goes, but Dad is leaving with her"

"No, Dad wouldn't leave your wedding, you must have misunderstood him."

No, Sara, I didn't and I don't care anymore, let him leave if he wants, apparently he has chosen Pat over me today, and I will never forgive him."

I walked out the door to go find Matt, I wasn't going to let Dad ruin my day, besides like he said he isn't my father.

Chapter thirteen

I moved into Matt's apartment, we decided to live there until we saved enough money to buy a house.

I hadn't heard from my Dad in seven months, so I guess he did feel like he wasn't my father, I did hear from Sara and Don, Sara told me that Pat controls his every move.

So I stopped calling and leaving messages on his voice mail.

I concentrated on being a good wife to Matt and that's all I cared about, his mother didn't accept me and I stopped letting that bother me also. Matt told me it was her loss and I agreed.

One year after our wedding, I became pregnant, we were so happy, even his mom was happy and started to talk to me in a civil way, and I knew she had always been disappointed that Matt married me, but now that she was going to be a grandmother, her whole attitude, and behavior toward me changed.

Matt and I didn't want to learn the sex of our child until it was born, but she was constantly after Matt to find out because she wanted to know, and I could see Matt giving in to her.

"Would it really hurt if we knew, that way we

could be ahead of the game because we would know what to buy pink or blue."

"Matt, I thought we had decided not to know"

"Okay, of course you are right and I don't want to know, I'm sorry I brought it up, my Mom is just driving me nuts, but she will have to wait."

"Thank you." I said, glad he was standing up to his mother.

The last two months of my pregnancy I was so miserable, it was midsummer, very hot, everything made me sick, my feet and hands were swollen.

Matt's workplace had their annual Independence day picnic, While I sat a picnic table in the hot shade without a breeze, Matt went to play baseball with his friends, promising me he would only play one game, then we could go home to my air-conditioned apartment and get out of this heat.

He had only been playing for about fifteen minutes when I felt something running down my leg , I realized my water had broken .

too embarrassed to stand up, I had to come up with another way to get Matt's attention.

There were two little girls also sitting at the table eating their lunch. "Hey sweetie, can you do me a favor please?" *I softly asked. They both just looked at me. "See that guy over there? the one with the red cap" Thankful he was the only one with a red cap.*

Will you go tell him that his wife needs him."

Without a word, she got up and started to walk toward Matt, but then she stopped and just stared at him, and I knew she was too shy to speak to a complete stranger, what was I thinking?

So I got up and walked toward him, he saw me and I waved for him to come.

The little girl walked back to the table and continued to eat as if nothing had happened.

Eight hours later I held my baby girl in my arms. She was the most beautiful thing I had ever seen, and my heart was overflowing with love. We named her Tara Ann.

Matt's mother had never been to our apartment until after the baby was born.

To me she acted like a very selfish grandmother right from the start, she wanted to be number one in her granddaughter's life, not sharing any time with anyone else, Tara was her only focus, and I would get very upset when she went against my wishes concerning my daughter, she showed me or her son no respect.

But I kept my mouth closed hoping Matt would address this big issue with his mother.

On Tara's first Birthday, my plans, I wanted just the three of us to go to the park with the small cake I had made for my daughter's birthday..

But my plans was overlooked when his mother decided to throw a one year old a birthday party that Tara would not understand or remember.

I went along with it because my husband asked me

too, not because I wanted too.

I knew how hard it was for him to say no to his Mom.

At the party there were more adults there than kids.

Grandma passed my baby around like a football.

Matt looked over at me, and I let him know it was time to go.

So he took the baby and said to his mother.

"Time for us to go, this little girl needs her nap"

We left with much protesting from his mom.

After that she was at our house every day, giving me unwanted instructions on how to raise my daughter.

Chapter Fourteen

I Had gotten Tara a little pumpkin costume for her first Halloween and she looked adorable.

I took lots off pictures for her baby book.

After supper Matt's mother called and begged Matt to bring the baby over so she could also take pictures of her in her costume.

Matt promised we wouldn't stay long.

During our visit, I noticed the dark clouds and I told Matt we should go, so we could get home before the storm started.

Shortly after putting Tara in her car seat she fell asleep.

"Matt, we need to set some boundaries with your mother, she totally ignored me when I told her the Tara could not have the chocolate."

"I know I will talk to her" I could see the storm was getting strong the winds were blowing hard and Matt was concentrating on driving so I didn't say anymore on the subject.

"I think we should have stayed at my mother's longer" he said.

That's when I saw out of the corner of my eyes kids just stepped off of the curve right in front of us, I remember screaming and being slammed up against the door.

The next thing I knew I was laying on the street

and the cold hard rain was hitting me in the face.

I lost my husband and my precious baby and my reasons for living that evening, I refused to talk about what happened to anyone.

I went through the emotions to do what had to be done.

people coming over to my mother -n –Law's house after the funeral.
didn't they know it took every ounce of my energy just to get through planning a funeral and now I have to have people over?
I know that everyone meant well, but having people here, some of them I barely knew, felt very unsettling.
And then came the inevitable questions,
Are you going to move? and what are you going to do now?
They act like they didn't really expect an answer,

which is exactly what they got, no reply, just a blank look.

Some offered comfort and pretend to understand even if they didn't. Other ones understood that I wanted to be left alone.

And then there were some that made me feel foolish for appearing vulnerable and weak.

I stayed with my sister because my whole family insisted I shouldn't be alone, and I knew I could not and would not ever go back into the apartment.

At my request they went to the apartment and packed up everything that pertained to only me, because I just couldn't make myself look at their things. They donated everything else

Matt's mother took to her bed and refused to be comforted.

After six months when all I did was laying around and cry my Dad insisted I talk to a psychologist so just to please him, I agreed I know peace for me was never to come again.

But I listened as Doctor Adams told me how I should feel.

"Ellen, It is normal to cry and be depressed, but you need to keep putting one foot in front of the other, just be Patient With yourself, you will not always feel the way you feel right now, you have took a hard blow, and your mind and your heart can't see pass that right now, and that's okay, you need time to heal.

There is no schedule time for when you should feel certain emotions, or be over the tragedy that you have suffered.

Every emotions that you are feeling right now is normal.

But one day, you will smile again."

To me the only good part about my sessions with Dr. Adams was after a while I could open up and talk about that night.

After six months I knew I had to get out of my sister's house, I was constantly being asked if I was Okay? by her and my niece & nephew and I could tell I was wearing out my welcome from Scott.

Chapter Fifteen

I decided I needed a change, to get away where no one knew me, no more sympathy looks from every one that I ran into.

I took what little saving we had left after paying for the funerals, and I rented an apartment eighty miles from my home town, It was very small and ran down but it was all I could afford..

I found a waitress job and settled into a routine. Worked every day, and cried myself to sleep every night.

I did continue to visit with Doctor Adams because he was the only person I wanted to talk to about what happened.

I knew he was getting paid to listen to me and for some reason that made a difference to me.

After telling Doctor Adams I had moved and gotten a job and wouldn't be making the long trip to see him anymore.

His reply was. "Ellen, it may seemed to you like you are making no progress, but I'm proud of you for making this giant step into your recovery it looks like you are finally getting your life back together."

I hated my Job, I hated my apartment and I hated my life without Matt and my baby, why did God take them and leave me behind to deal with it? My life had no meaning anymore.

My boss at work was constantly trying to get me to laugh or smile, he said I was hurting his business and I did try to fake it, when I would wait on customers, but somedays I would forget so I got hollered at a lot.

"Ellen, I'm sorry but I have hired another waitress to take your place," "Why would you do that? You know how much I need this job."
"I'm sorry, but I have got so many complaints about you and your composure you always seem irritable toward your customers, and you never smile, I have a business to run and lately you have been running customers away, I have an opening

for a dishwasher in the back if you want it the job is yours."

"You know I can't make a living as a dishwasher, that won't even pay my rent." "Like I said I'm sorry Ellen, It's all I have."

" What if I changed?" I pleaded. "No Ellen, that is what you told me last time we had this same conversation, I warned you, I'm sorry, Ellen."

That night lying on my couch, I wondered why I was still living, what was the point?" I truly had no one, Dad was so wrapped up in Pat, and he wouldn't even answer my phone calls anymore. Sara couldn't even help herself, and Don had his own life and no one else seem to matter to him anymore.

But I knew I couldn't make it as a dishwasher, so I would have to find another job, the only experience I had was waitressing.

The next morning, I walked down to the corner store and got a newspaper, I couldn't waste any time, my rent was coming due in three days.

After making myself the last of my coffee, I turned to the want ads; it was slim pickings for me, because everything was requiring some experience.

Just when I was about to give up an ad caught my eye.

WANTED, TRAVELING COMPANION.

Looking for a female companion to travel with an elderly woman.

All expense paid, with a monthly salary, must pass a criminal and drug test, if you love to travel call Mary ....

Wow, what an amazing job that would be, with the odds stacked against me, I dialed the number given.

"Good Afternoon Ramsey's resident." "Hi, can I speak to Mary, please" "Mrs., Ramsey is not taking calls today, can I help you?" "Yes, well I hope so; I'm calling about the ad in the paper." "And you are?" "Oh I'm sorry my name is Ellen." "Hi Ellen, because of the many inquiries about the ad that Mrs. Ramsey posted, I'm afraid at this

point, she has as many responds as she can handle right now, but if you would like to leave your phone number, I will make sure Mrs. Ramsey received it." "Oh, okay, thank you," I knew he could hear the disappointment in my voice.

After giving the man my phone number, I hung up. My heart was so heavy, but I should have known I could never get a job like that.

Chapter Sixteen

The next morning, I called every restaurant in the surrounding area, just hoping one would be needing a waitress, I had two days to come up with the rest of my rent money, I had too much pride to call my family.

That night once again I took out the photo album, it didn't bring me peace it brought me hurt but I just needed to see their faces tonight.

I had every one of the photos in order.

A picture of my high school graduation, a picture of me and my beautiful mother, looking at that picture now I could see she was sick, my brother and sister, and then Me and Matt's wedding, he was so handsome in his tux, my grown was beautiful and my eyes were bright, not like now, photos of when Matt carried me across the threshold of our apartment, I never did figure out who took that picture, and then a picture of me pregnant with Tara, this is where the tears usually would start to fall.

Matt in the delivery room dressed in his hospital uniform.

He looked so happy and then the picture of Matt holding his newborn daughter, that day was so joyful. There were pictures of us as a family, Tara's first Birthday party at his Mother's, the one I was against.

Matt and Tara were my world, I missed them so much I prayed every night for god to let me see them in my dreams, to hold my baby again and to feel Matt's arms around me just one more time, but the dreams never came, without the photos I was forgetting what they looked like.

Doctor Adams told me to give myself time to accept what has happened, but how do I do that? How do I accept what had happened? When I can never see my little girl grow up or ever see my husband again?

Choose to move on, he told me.

But he doesn't have to figure out how he is going to get through the rest of his life.

It was easy for him to say that to me, he wasn't the one that lost his family in a blink of an eye; he still has his wife and his children to go home to, after he told me to let it go.

The next day, I didn't even want to get out of bed, I just wanted to lay there and remember my life with Matt trying to keep every little moment in my memory, lest I forget.

The ringing of my phone brought me back to the present. "Hello" "Hello, may I speak to Ellen, please"
"Speaking" I said into the phone.
"Hi Ellen, you had required about a companion job?" My heart skipped a beat... "Yes sir" "would you be available tomorrow afternoon to come in for an interview?" "Yes sir that would be great"
I tried to hide my enthusiasm, but I couldn't.

"Fine, Mary will see you at three pm"
after giving me the address, I thanked him, and then we hung up.

I fell to my knees and I prayed to god to have mercy on me and please give me this job.
I had a hard time sleeping that night, I was so worried that I wouldn't get this much needed, much wanted job.
It could change so much for me, I could travel and then maybe I could take Doctor Adams advice that my Dad paid dearly for.

"Choose to stand up for yourself, and don't try to plan out the rest of your life, Just focus on one day at a time, and you might be surprised to see that tomorrow came and went easy for you.
Ellen, believe me One day you will not look back but you will look forward."
I prayed Dr. Adams was right.

Chapter Seventeen

I Told the cab driver the address, and became a little worried when he gave me a funny look, I was hoping he wasn't going into a bad part of town.

But I got a very pleasant surprised when He turned down one of the wealthiest street I had ever seen, my hope soared.

When he stopped in front of a big beautiful house

to me was more like a mansion I was almost too scared to walk on the pavement.

I was a bundle of nerves to say the least.

A real life butler answered the door and right away I recognized his voice when he spoke, as the man that had called me.

"Hi Ellen,?" "Yes" I nervously said.

"Come in please, I will let Mary, I mean Mrs. Ramsey know you are here."

"Thank you" I stood there on shaky knees because he didn't offer me a seat, which I wish he had.

But in just a few minutes he was back.

"You can come this way, would you like something to drink?" "No thank you" I politely said. We went into a big beautiful room that looked like a liberty, I felt like I was on the game Clue.

Mrs. Ramsey was definitely not what I was expecting she was just a very older sweet lady.

She had a kind voice and I immediately liked her. I thought she would be like one of those ladies with a fake blond wig and two tight clothes , and a little yapping dog with an expensive collar on.

“Hi Ellen, please sit down dear,

Edward, get this girl something to drink please,

we have a lot to talk about.”

I sat in one of the chairs that faced her.

“Ellen, would you mind telling me about yourself?”

“Sure, I graduated high school, I had planned on going to college, but my mother became ill, and I decided not to go.”

“Oh I’m sorry, I hope it was nothing serious”

her voice held true sympathy.

“My mother passed away just three days before I was to leave for college. “Oh I’m so very sorry”

“Thank you” “Are you working right now?”

“I was until just a few days ago; I was looking for

another job, when I came across your ad."

"I see. What kind of job did you have?"

" I was a waitress" I started to shake. "Honey, don't be nervous, I don't bite"

I knew if I wanted this job, I was going to have to start talking.

"Mrs. Ramsey, I want this job so badly and I'm sure out of all the girls that you have interviewed have more experience and more work ethics than me, but I promise you there is not one that needs this job or deserves it more than me.

And I give you my promise I will do my very best to do a great job for you."

I couldn't hold the tears in any longer. She just looked at me for a long time while I waited to be dismissed, I stopped crying and I became very upset with myself.

"Mrs. Ramsey, I'm so sorry, I think it was just my nerves, I had been anticipating this interview all day.

"Well Ellen, we have to get one thing straight right now, I refuse to travel and spent hours with someone as my travel companion that doesn't call me by my given name and that is Mary, so no more Mrs. Ramsey Okay."

I looked up at her in shock. "Okay" I said..

"Do you live with your dad?" she asked.

"No I have an apartment" "Will you be able to leave it?" "Oh yes, yes I will" my heart was pounding.

"My driver will come for you tomorrow at noon."

"Thank you so much, I promise you won't be sorry for giving me this chance."

"No, I don't believe I will." She smiled at me.

I walked out of her home after giving Edward my address.

I had no idea how I was getting home and I didn't even care.

I walked a ways away before I called a cab.

As soon as I got home I started to pack my things, I wonder where we would go first?

I didn't care about where it was.

I was just so happy to be leaving this place.

I laid in bed that night and again I thought about Doctor Adams words. "Ellen you don't have to figure out how you're going to get through the rest of your life, just live one day at a time."

Chapter Eighteen

The next morning I called my landlady, and my sister and I left a message on my Dad's answering machine, I told them about my new job.

My sister, but not my landlady were happy for me.

I was ready when the Limo came to my shaggy apartment complex to escort me to Mary's.

I didn't know all the job requirements, but I was going to do my best to fulfill them, as I unpack my things in the room that was bigger than my apartment, I said ..... "Thank you god for giving me this job, and please forgive me for being mad at you for so long." Edward had giving me a form to fill out and when I was done with it; Mary would go over my duties with me. He said.

An hour later I was following Edward down a long corridor, Mary was waiting on the sofa for me. "Hi Ellen, did you get settled in?" "Yes, thank you, the room is beautiful." "Well if you ever need anything, Edward will take care of you." "Thank you." "So Ellen, I take it that you like to travel" "Yes I do, but I just never had the opportunity to do so." "If you could travel anywhere, in the world, where would you go?"

"That's easy, Paris" "Oh why Paris?" "Ever since I

was a little girl, I had dreamed of going to Paris in high school I worked as a waitress and saved every dime I could, to go there after Graduation with two of my best friends before we headed off to college, and I have kept my passport updated, because I wanted to hang on to my childhood dream,"

"What stopped you from going?" Like I said, my mom got sick and I had to cancel because I couldn't leave her." "I'm sorry."

"Before Mr. Ramsey passed, we traveled to Paris, once a year, we have indeed traveled just about everywhere you can think, that was our life, so when he became ill, our traveling stopped.

But now I'm ready to pick it back up, but since we were never blessed with children of our own,

I do not like to travel alone, so that is where you come in, to be my traveling buddy, all of your expense will be paid, and a nice salary for your time.

We will dine at the best restaurants and we will stay at the best luxury hotels, you will accompany me to many fancy mingles and operas."

"It all sounds so exciting" I said.

"Oh it is my dear" I have made an appointment for you tomorrow morning to be fitted for your new wardrobe and at my personal hairdresser." "

"Thank you so much Mary, this is all very exciting to me."

"I'm excited as well to be out there again mingling with my friends, I have always lived the fast life and I miss it."

I was very glad I still had my figure so I wouldn't be embarrassed when people were putting clothes on me.

I had butterflies in my stomach and once again, I said Thank you God for giving me this Job.

After I dined with Mary and Edward, I went to my very own private bathroom and soaked in a tub big enough to swim in.

I wondered what they would do to my hair tomorrow, not that I cared.

She could have said they were shaving my head and I would have done it.

My hair was kept on the long side just layered and styled I loved it, I had only one manicure and pedicure in my life and that was when my friend's mom got us three girls one for our prom.

I loved being pampered like this.

When they started bringing out beautiful evening

gowns like the ones I used to look at in magazines when I was a child, I knew, we weren't going to Branson Missouri.

The clothes that were carried out to that Limo that day were fit for a queen. There were boxes of shoes and hats. Edward told me not to worry too much. I would also get the opportunity to shop for myself; But I wasn't worried at all. Back at the house after all my things were put into my room, I had lunch with Mary. "Did you like the things you got today?" "Oh my yes, everything was so beautiful, I can't wait to wear them. " Good, I'm glad you are pleased.

"Ellen, in our interview, I didn't really have the chance to really get to know about you, you had mention that you needed this job more than anyone else, why is that? Because you don't strike

me as someone that is in it for the money, and since we will be together a lot and you will be living in my house, I want to know all about you, if you don't mind."

" No I don't mind

My Dad remarried two years after my mom's passing and the woman he married didn't want him to have anything to do with his kids, so over the years we have drifted apart, I have a brother in the Army his name is Don and he is four years older than me, I have a sister, Sara she is two years older, she is married and has two children. Almost three years after I graduated. I married the love of my life, his name was Matt, and he was my soul mate."

" You talk about him as if in past tense?" Mary said. "Yes he was killed in a car accident along

with our fifteen month old daughter." "Oh my goodness, honey I'm so sorry"

My world was forever changed on that night three years ago. "Oh Ellen, you don't have to tell me the details, I can see this conversation is hard on you." "No it's okay; grief has taught me that sometimes I don't have to let it go. I just have to let it out. I have held it in for so long, I think it may be good to tell someone other than my Doctor. Mary reached and took my hand.

It was Halloween, we took Tara, that's my baby girl's name to Matt's parent's house to show off her little pumpkin costume, we didn't stay long because the weather was turning stormy and we wanted to get home and get Tera in bed. I still to this day don't know why the parents of those boys let them be out in the storm trick or treating, they should have been inside a shelter, and the storm was getting worst. I remember the last words Matt spoke. "   "We should have stayed at Mom's," then I heard screams and brakes and glass and wind, when I came to, I was lying on a the wet pavement, it was raining so hard and it was so cold, I tasted water and blood in my mouth, I was screaming for Matt, that's when I saw Tara's car seat it was upside down, I crawled as fast as I could to her, there was a boy lying close to the car seat and I screamed for him to help me, but he didn't move, I was able to get Tara out of the car seat, I heard people yelling, I heard the police sirens , I held Tara trying to shelter her from the cold rain, she wasn't crying, thank god she slept through it, I thought., I turned around so I could lean against the car because I was in so much pain, that is when I saw Matt, he was lying in the middle of the road, I watched as paramedics started working on him. Than a lady was talking to me, even though she was real close to me, I couldn't hear what she was saying to me, she reached out to take Tara from arms. "No I screamed, I held her tight, it seemed after I screamed I could hear. "Let me check her to make sure she is okay" she said, so I gave her Tara, then I laid down for just a little while, I remember thinking. When I awoke all I could see was bright lights , and a doctor was saying my name over and over, I saw my Dad standing behind the Doctor, but I was so sleepy, I couldn't keep my eyes open. I was told later that I had cerebral edema; I had bleeding inside my brain because of the head trauma I had suffered. I had been in and out of a coma; I had two surgeries that I knew nothing about. My head had been shaved and I had been in this bed for six weeks. It was my Dad that told me that Matt and Tera didn't make it, all I could do was scream, when the haunting memories started to come back it was torture to my heart. Every night my mind replayed the horrible ordeal that I would never forget. I watched as paramedics tried to breathe life back into my husband, while another paramedic spoke words of comfort to me as I held my lifeless baby girl in my arms. Trying to convince me to release her into her care, only seconds had past, but to me it was a lifetime.

My Dad and sister and my brother tried to comfort me., but I couldn't be comforted. The days turned into weeks, I stayed at my sister's house, but I couldn't stand it there, I was constantly being asked if I was okay? I thought the day had come that I wanted to know what had happened to my husband and my daughter but I was very wrong. They told me, Tara had died on impact when she was in my arms she was dead. Matt died on the way to the hospital; one of the young boys that had run out in front of us was also killed. Matt hit a big tree trying to miss hitting the boy but he hit them both then lost control of the car according to the other two boys that witness the whole thing... I know this may sound strange but ever since that evening I can't forgive myself, I feel guilty for being alive."   "Oh honey, can't you see the good lord kept you alive for a reason, I'm a strong believer that everyone has their own date, and it wasn't your time that day, and God must have not wanted Matt to go alone so he took his daughter, but you mustn't feel guilty for living, but instead you should embrace life every day."   "I will try to see it that way, I know this job is going to help me." "Good, if you ever need to talk, I will be here for you, I want to help you get your life back on track, life is too short for to feel guilt, So what happened after that?"

Matt and I had only rented a place we were saving to buy our own house, so when I couldn't take staying at my sister's place anymore, I took what little money we had saved and I rented the apartment eighty miles from my sister's and the place I had grown up in, trying to put the past behind me but trauma of losing them is always just one step behind me. I got another waitress job, but I couldn't be the happy go lucky girl my boss needed, it just wasn't in me, because I was carrying too much heartache and guilt, I have often wondered why didn't God just take me that night also. So anyway to make a long story short I was forced to become a dishwasher, and I knew I couldn't make money to live on so I started looking for another job, I had wanted for a long time to embarked on a new career and thanks to you, I'm going to be okay now." Mary had tears in her eyes. "You are so young and yet you have been through more than an old person like me has went through, don't ever think you are not a strong person, you are very strong and I'm so happy, you found my ad that day."   " Oh Mary, so am I," I said. "Ellen, get a good night's sleep because tomorrow morning, we are on our way to Paris." "Are you serious? Just like that we can go to Paris?" " Just like that," She laughed.

Chapter Nineteen

When we arrived at the Hotel, I started to carry some of our luggage in, but the door greeter stopped me.

"Ellen, that is not your job Dear," Mary informed me. I felt foolish, but I didn't have a clue to what my job was? My eyes were filled with stars, I

didn't think it was possible for Paris to be more beautiful than what it was in my head, but it was. We were staying at the Le Grand and it was breathtaking, I had seen pictures of this Hotel in the many magazines all about Paris, but I would have never in a million years ever thought I would even get close to the property that it sat on, and here I am as a guest. Once we were settled in our suite,

Mary wanted to rest from our trip, but I couldn't rest, I wanted to see everything in this grand Hotel. She told me to go and explore, and that is what I did. It had been over three years since I had felt this kind of joy and I wanted to hang on to it before it all vanished. When I returned to our suite hours later, I was tired but very happy I had taken many pictures to share with Sara.

That evening we dined in the ballroom, there is no way to describe the elegant beauty that my eyes beheld. I felt like a princess as I was swayed on the dance floor by an older gentleman, a friend of Mary's my long grown was also very beautiful I looked like I fit right in, but I knew if I opened my mouth, they would know I didn't, I didn't know how to speak their rich language, But I wanted to be like them, I wanted to really fit in, to talk and to act like them.

When Mary and I returned to our suite, I asked her if one day she would teach me. "Teach you what? Dear." "How to be elegant." I said. She laughed. "Don't you know? You are already elegant and beautiful?" " But I want to know how to act, when I'm around other people." " You mean rich people?"

" Yes, I guess that is what I'm saying."

" That's easy, just be a snob, No I'm joking, the only thing I can tell you is that a woman appears to be elegant by the way she carries herself, her posture, an elegant woman speaks confidence about things she knows, she has class and appreciation for the finer things and of course having a great figure doesn't hurt. She gave me a wink.

Chapter Twenty

The next day I got to go on my first yacht with Mary and her friend, and it was everything I could have dreamed it would be. I met an old friend of Mary's that quite frankly I got the impression he wanted to be more than her friend. At least that was my thinking when she introduced us. "Well hello Ellen, so you are Mary's traveling companion? This lady will definitely wear you out, I hope you are ready for the challenge." " Oh I think I am. I'm having a blast." Well good, have you been to Paris before?" " No this is my first time."

" You just look so familiar."

" James, are you trying to pick up my girl?" Mary jokingly said.

"Now Mary, you know there is no other girl for me than you." After they walked away, I knew my intertwisting was right and that made me a little worried; what if they got married, then she wouldn't need me anymore. "Hi, you must be Mrs. Ramsey's traveling partner? She told us she was getting someone to travel with her." I looked up into sea blue eyes and got all tongue tied. He gave out a nervous laugh when I didn't say anything I'm sure he got the impression that I rather not

speak to anyone. "I'm sorry to bother you, have a good day" He walked away. Well maybe I can act like the rich I just pulled off being a big snob. I had to find him and apologize for my rudeness. But it was a big ship, and I couldn't see him anywhere.

That evening as Mary and I went to the dining area to have supper with James and a few of Mary's friend, The man I was rude to was also seated at our table.. Mary introduced us. "Lucas, this is Ellen, Lucas is James's only son, can't you tell, they favor a lot. "Lucas stood to his feet; well we kind of already met earlier on the top deck. "I'm so sorry about that, you caught me off guard." "Oh that is fine." He acted like he could care less so I dropped it, and enjoyed my evening... A little while later Lucas asked me to dance. "You look familiar to me, but I can't seem to place you." "That's funny, your father said the same thing when he met me, I guess I just have that certain face that looks like everyone else." He put his head back and laughed. "Let me reassure you my dear, you may have the face that every girl wishes they had, I have a feeling they broke the mold after this creation." "I'm not sure if that was a complement or you just insulted me... " He laughed then picked me up and swung me around on the dance floor. I had a feeling that Lucas was a very fun guy. We danced every song;

I was having so much fun with Lucas. Mary excused herself to return to her cabin. I knew it was my job to escort her, even though she insisted I stay and enjoy myself. As we walked down the long hall, I held her arm. "Are you enjoying yourself Child?" "Oh yes Mary, I am, thank you so much for making my dreams come true." "You are welcome, this is just the beginning."

That night I laid in bed and I tried to see Matt's face, but Lucas's face kept appearing.

How could I even think about planning for a future without Matt and Tara? I knew I had to get Lucas out of my head he didn't belong there.

What would Matt think of me if he knew I was thinking about someone else? I knew Matt and Tara were gone forever and I knew they were never coming back, I also knew I could never replace them, my baby girl is gone and after three years my tears may have dried, and I can probably utter her name without breaking apart, but I will never forget her, or the feel of her warm body in my arms as I rocked her to sleep so many times, again I asked god to please let them visit me in my dreams.

Chapter Twenty One

I Didn't understand how Mary could keep up with everything, I mean she wasn't really old but she seemed feeble, like a china doll that could break. Almost every other evening we were at a big party with wealthy people at the most incredible beautiful places. I know Lucas could have any girl he wanted but he seem to want to spend his time with me and I didn't complain. He was charming, and because of him I was seeing so much of Paris while I was here, I knew if not for him I wouldn't have. It did start to worry me that I was having feelings for him that I knew I shouldn't. Lucas and I came from two different worlds.

I already knew I wasn't the only one developing feelings for someone, I saw as James and Mary became very friendly, I was a little confused about James's intentions, because I very pretty sure Mary even though she didn't look like it, because she carried herself with such grace and charm but still she had to be old enough to be his mother, but I guess Paris knows no age boundaries when it comes to love..

I wasn't surprised when one evening she told me that he had proposed.

"Ellen, James has asked me to marry him," "Oh Mary, I'm so happy for you" "I turned him down" "Oh" I didn't know what to say to that. "My late Husband and I made a promise to each other that neither of us would ever remarry if one of us should pass." "I see" I sadly said. I felt so sorry for her because that was a promise that never should have been made. "Mary, it is certainly none of my business but don't you think that was an unfair promise on both of your parts, I know how much you love your late husband, but he is gone and you are still here, and your heart was made to love more than just one person at a time. I think you are in love with James, am I wrong?" " No you are not wrong, and James put up that same argument, but how can I break that promise."

"Just ask him, and God to forgive you." I said. "Could it be that easy?" She said. "I know James loves you very much, and you love him."

I knew if they got married, she wouldn't need my services anymore, but she deserved happiness with James.

The next morning, Mary went with James, so I decided to walk around the grounds of this big magnificent hotel. When I was dressed in jeans and top, I opened the door to find Lucas just about to ring the bell. "Lucas, you startled me" "I am very sorry, I came to ask you if you would like to go sightseeing with me?" "I would love too; it will only take a minute to change my clothes"

"No what you have on is perfect." "Are you sure?" "I'm very sure." He laughed.

The first place he took me was the Eiffel tower where we ended up staying for the entire day and I loved it. We went to the modern art museum, we attended an art show, and the sight was so beautiful I wanted to stay there forever... "I love your enthusiasm about the littlest things." He smiled at me. "The Eiffel tower is not little. I laughed."

That night I tried again to see Matt's face but Lucas's face kept coming into my mind and it made me feel guilty like I had done something wrong, how could I, tell Mary to move on when I couldn't..." I had to forget about Lucas because as soon as Mary and James married I would be back in the states and back to my boring life, but I was still so thankful to Mary and to God for giving me this grand opportunity to get to come to Paris, and to get to more than fulfill my lifetime dream.

Chapter Twenty Two

One week later, Mary informed me we would be leaving for home at the end of the month, I knew she had been bothered by something, but I didn't feel like I had a right to ply into her affairs, so I waited until she wanted to talk to me.

But I was heart sick to be leaving. "I will turn in early tonight, James has had me doing so many different things I'm afraid I'm wearing out fast, but I'm sure you will find some amusement of enjoyment this evening." "I can stay with you, if you would like" "Oh no, Call Lucas, go and enjoy yourself, there is only two weeks before we leave, so take advantage of it." "Okay, thank you Mary, rest well." I didn't tell her that Lucas had already asked me to dinner tonight, but I never make plans until I find out what her plans are. I called Lucas and told him I was free tonight. I knew we had been seeing a lot of each other and I have grown very fond of him, but like Mary said this dream was going to end in two weeks. He took me to Le cinq it was very romantic. I hadn't realize just how much I had fallen for Lucas over these past three weeks until tonight when he held me in his arms as we danced. I kept telling myself that I was leaving soon and most likely would never see him again but my heart wouldn't listen to reasoning, instead it ached at that thought.

I knew I would always love Matt, he was placed in that part of my heart with Tara that no one could touch or take away. But somehow Lucas had found his way in to my heart also and caused me to fall in love again, it was such a happy feeling after being so unhappy for so long.

We spend every minute we could together, he was an amazing man. "Tell me about your family, I asked him one day while we were sitting out on the balcony. "Not much to tell I was born here, my father and his father and so on comes from wealth." "What about your mother?" "My mother divorced my father and now lives in Italy;
I don't see much of her." He said. "Lucas, why haven't you ever married?" "Well that's an easy question, I just hadn't met you yet"
he softly kissed me and all of my other questions were soon forgotten.

Over the next few days Mary took sick and stayed in her bed, I stayed with her until she felt better, Lucas came every evening, and we dined in the hotel banquet. "Ellen, something has happened."
"What? I got worried right away."
" I have fallen in love with you." Those words made my heart sing. "I'm in love with you too Lucas, but next week I will be leaving."
"Don't go" "Lucas, even though that would be the logic answer, I was hired to be Mrs. Ramsey's traveling companion, I have to go back."
"She will understand if you decide to stay." he said.
"I just can't do that to her, I'm sorry." "Are you saying we should toss our love aside?" "No I want to be with you Lucas, I will talk to Mary."

That night I cried just thinking about leaving Lucas, I wanted to be with him, but I couldn't afford to live in Paris on my own, I had to go back with Mary, she has been so good to me and I loved my job. Here I wouldn't have a place to live or a job, I know Lucas has never worried about things like that, but it has been my constant worry since Matt died.

Lucas called me the next morning to see how Mary was feeling, "She is feeling much better, in fact your father is picking her up in just a little while." "That's great news, because I want to take you to a place, you haven't seen yet." "That's sounds great." I said.

I was hoping to talk to Lucas today and tell him I would be leaving with Mary, and hope he wouldn't ask me too many questions, because I didn't want to start crying again today.

"I will pick you up in an hour."

He held my hand as we walked at the square du Vert- Galant, we sat and watched the boats. "It is beautiful here." I said as I laid my head on his shoulder. Lucas stood up and knelt down on his knee, I thought for sure my heart was going to jump out of my chest. "Ellen, I have met lots of woman but none of them has ever stolen my heart like you have, I can't even begin to image my life without you in it, I love you, and I'm asking you to be my wife." Then he took out of his pocket a beautiful ring that I know must had cost him a small fortune. "Lucas, you gave me joy that I thought I would never have again, I will marry you, because I love you and I can't image leaving and never seeing you again." My heart was so overflowing, and I knew Mary would be happy for me. Marrying Lucas was the only way I could stay and be with him, there would be no way I could live here on my own, his proposal changed my life. I would be with the man I loved and live in the place that I loved.

Chapter Twenty Four

There is going to be a Banquet dinner tomorrow night to honor my father, I would like to make our announcement then.

"Lucas are you sure, wouldn't that be taken away from your father? it is his night." "No this will give him joy, it is our family culture to make a big announcement here, and this is very big to me, because I have found the love of my life, so it will be our secret until then."

That night it was hard not to tell Mary, not only of the engagement, but I needed to tell her I would no longer be going back with her.

"Ellen, tomorrow evening we both are invited to a dinner in honor of James, This will give you an opportunity to wear one of the lovely evening gowns. I couldn't deceive Mary, I had to tell her.

"Mary, I need to talk to you about something."

"What is it dear?" Today, Lucas ask me to marry him and I said yes."

" Oh Ellen, that is marvelous, Lucas is a great man, I'm so happy for you, now your dream will take a big turn, you won't just visit Paris, you will live in Paris." She seemed as excited as I was"

"So you are not disappointed that I will not be returning back with you." "Of course I will be

disappointed, but I would never stand in the way of love, and I am truly happy for you, after everything you have gone through, this is perfect, you come to Paris and find love, and I'm glad I was a part of it." "You are not just a big part of it, but you are the reason for it and I will be forever grateful to you." "Oh this is a celebration!" she said.....

I loved dressing up in the beautiful gowns, I felt so elegant just like the ladies in the magazines. I would spend hours looking at and daydreaming that it was me. And now it was me. "Oh wow, you definitely look like you belong in Paris" Mary said as I stepped in the room. "Thank you Mary, such kind words." "True words, you are beautiful, my dear, inside and out."

From Lucas I got a wink and a smile so I took that is a positive response. "Shall we?" He offered me his arm to escort me to the waiting Limo. I was very anxious when we entered the room I had never in my life seen such elegance and beauty before, it was breathtaking, but for some reason I didn't feel out of place just the contrary, I felt like this is where I belonged. I was proud to be on Lucas's arm as we mingled with very wealthy people I'm sure. So far no one I had met were snobs just the opposite, I overheard some women talking about recipes, which was kind of a letdown, shouldn't they be discussing fashion and their trips to Rome.

After the ceremony for James was over, Lucas went up in front of all the people and tapped his wine glass. "May I have your attention please, I'm very proud of my father and I only hope one day, I can fill his footstep." But tonight I would like to let everyone know including my father that I have asked this beautiful lady"

He motion for me to join him,

I walked up and stood by his side,

and he continued. To be my wife and she has said yes." Everyone cheered; his father came and gave me a hug. "This is a very nice surprise." People I didn't know congratulated us. I felt like the queen of the Ball and I loved it.

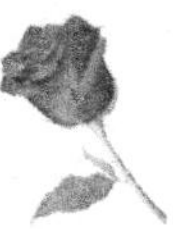

Chapter Twenty Five

The next day I couldn't keep my great news in, so I called Sara and told her everything, she was so excited for me. "Sara, please say you will come for the wedding." "Oh Ellen, I don't know if that is possible for me to come that far." She sounded worried. "Sara you won't have to pay for anything, please promise that you will think about it." "I promise I will think about it." Sara and I were so totally different from each other. She settled for whatever was handed to her, but I had always wanted more, I had always wanted what I couldn't have. Mother had told me that her sister Riley always wanted to run to other places, and experience the finer things in life. Was I like her? My birth Mother? I didn't know. But one thing, I did know I would have never left my daughter behind.

Lucas wanted to start planning our wedding right away; he said it would be a grand event. I was very excited to see how my wedding would turn out. We both agree on a Christmas wedding. Right away he hired a French wedding planner, Lucas knew him, but I hadn't met him yet. Mary had extended her stay here in Paris for another month to attend our engagement party; it seemed to me as everything was moving very fast, but that is how it's been ever since we have arrived in Paris.

Chapter Twenty Six

Lucas and I were together every day, and every day I fell more in love with him, I loved being on his arm in my lovely grown as he introduced me as his fiancé, and to see the envy on every single girl's face.

I was living the life I had always dreamed of and as much as I loved Lucas, I still loved and

Missed Matt and I always would. When I arrived back at our suite Mary was still up.

"Mary, how are you, I have been so busy, and I haven't had a chance to catch my breath." I laughed. "I am fine dear; I know it is very exciting to be marrying one of the wealthy eligible bachelors." "I know I have to pinch myself sometime, I mean you know where I came from I was just a peasant." "You were never just a peasant more like a very beautiful Cinderella that was waiting for her prince, and like you told me that day about this Job, no one deserves it more than you." "Thank you, so what is going on with you and James?" "James and I have decided to remain friends." She said. "I was so hoping to

have you as my mother." "That is very sweet of you to say, but I will always be your friend."

Chapter Twenty Seven

I Knew the engagement party was going to be a big event with people I did not know, but it didn't matter, I was anxious and excited as the hairdresser put my long hair up in a very stylish Paris doo. The party would be held at my soon to be father-n-law's mansion, the same mansion that would be my new home. As the limo pulled up behind many other limos, Lucas was waiting outside for me, looking stunning in his tux. The house was everything I had expected it to be, elegant and beautiful. The night passed too quickly for me. After the majority of the quests had left, Lucas took me on a tour of the estate; every room was more breathtaking than the other. In the liberty where Lucas took me into arms and kissed me was my favorite room, not just because of the kiss but because of the history and the art, and I could tell this room was one of the most used rooms in the house, I could faintly smell the odor of a fine cigar, that still lingered in the room, the furniture was a rich brown leather, it was the idea place to spend a productive afternoon away from the noisiness of the busy city. Above the fireplace hung a very large portrait of a beautiful woman, she looked graceful and very petite in a long blue grown. Lucas came up behind me and put his arms around me. "Who is the lovely lady?" I asked as I nested my head on his chest. "Mother." "She is very beautiful." I said. "Yes she is a looker, shall we continue our tour?" "Yes", I answered.

Upstairs on the long hallway wall were a lot more photography's and as Lucas was telling me who they all were of, my eyes fixed on a photo of a woman standing with his Father. "Lucas who is this woman?" "The same woman you just seen in the Liberty." "What is her name?" "Victoria." He answered. My mind was going in every direction, this was definitely a picture of Riley, my mother, and I felt sick to my stomach, there were many photos of her. "Lucas, I don't feel so well, I think I need to go back to the Hotel. "What's wrong?" he sounded concerned." " Just a headache" I lied. "Okay, I will take you back." "No, there are still guest here, you stay, just have someone drive me please." "Are you sure?" "Yes, I'm very sure"

I just needed to get out of there and quickly.

In the Limo, I couldn't hold my tears back. Mt fairytale dream just ended and my heart was so broken, I couldn't believe I was deeply in love with my own Brother and almost married him. Now I was ready to leave Paris for good.

Chapter Twenty Eight

The next Morning, I just had to have some answers, I was up all night thinking about, what if I was wrong, what if she just looks identical to my real mother, everyone has a double, the only thing that gave me hope was her name was Victoria and My mother's name is Riley.

I prayed that Mary could tell me something about Lucas's mother.

I didn't even take time to shower or dress. She was at the table having her morning coffee, She hadn't been looking good the last couple of days and I hated to disturbed her, but I had no one to turn to. "Mary, are you feeling up to talking?" "Of course dear, what's on your mind?" "Mary can you tell me about James and Victoria?" "James and Victoria?" she looked confused. "What would you like to know?" "How they met?" I said because I didn't know where to start. "That is a strange story, but I guess some people could say, it was a love story." "Oh, really? How so?" " James told me when he was younger, he was on a cruise ship that had eighty eight more passengers aboard when the ship mysteriously capsized, and thirty nine people lost their lives that day. But

Victoria was one of them that had survive, she was found four days later, James said she was thrown up against the rocks, she had multiple injuries, damage to her Bain and her spleen, she was hospitalize, when she came to, she didn't know where she was, or what had happened to her, James said she didn't know who she was, not even her name, the poor thing."

" So how did she get the name Victoria?" He said he gave her that name just because she looked like a Victoria, and because she didn't know her own name, and he had to call her something so he started calling her Victoria and it just stuck... "So how did James become involved with her in the first place?" I was still confessed. "James joined the search party and he was the one who found her, and during all the time he spent at the hospital with her, they fell in love. The doctor had

told both of them that one day her memory could come back. But they didn't want to wait so they both took the chance that she was free to marry so they married, despite the fact that he was much older than her. Years later when her memory did start to come back to her, James said because she was so free spirited and couldn't stand to be tied down, she left him and it broke his heart. Victoria was a beauty," Mary said. "Yeah I know." "I take it, you have seen her portrait in the liberty? " "Yes, I did." "That is one of the reason that I have decided James and I can only be friends, because he is still in love with her, and he informed me her picture would never be took down"

"I'm sorry Mary"

I knew I had to explain to her why I couldn't marry Lucas and why I wanted to go home. "Mary, I have to tell you my whole story, when I saw photos of Victoria, I knew that she was my mother." "I don't understand you told me your mother died"

"Let me start from the beginning. Before my mother passed away, her and my father called me into her room and told me shocking news, they told me that my mother's younger sister Riley ran off with a man and when she returned she was pregnant with me and she was going to put me up for adoption so the two people I had believed all my life were my parents took me and raised me as their own, my mother told me her sister left right after I was born and they never seen or heard from her again, they got word years later that she had drown, my mother never told me if she knew

where, just that she had passed, my father told me that my mom suffered many nights not knowing where or what had happened to her sister."

"Oh my goodness, that is horrible, so you think that Victoria is your mother?"

" Yes now more than ever, I have her photos with my things at your house, I just want to go home."

I begin to cry again. "Oh honey, what did Lucas say?" "I didn't tell him and I'm not going too, I will just go home and sent him a message that I had changed my mind about marrying him and then I will never see him again." "But Ellen is that really fair to him?" "Mary, I just can't tell him, I just want to go home." "Okay, we will go home, I will also sent James a message after we return and tell him we left because of my health, which will almost be the truth, I haven't been feeling good these last few days." "Thank you Mary." She called someone and I heard her speak into the phone......"Please make our arrangements we will be departing first thing in the morning for home."

That night I was so exhausted from no sleep the previous night, the wee hours of the morning, sleep finally took over.

Chapter Twenty Nine

Once back home I tried to put Lucas and Parris out of my mind, I was also trying to come to the conclusion that my girlish dreams were just dreams and they needed to be put in my past, I don't belong in Paris and I don't belong with wealthy people, I am who I am, whither I liked it or not, which was okay, I knew I would have to get over Lucas, he is my brother and I would not allow myself to have any kind of thoughts about him other than my brother that I would never see again.

Mary stayed in bed a lot since we arrived back. The doctor was in a few times, I was worried about her.

It had been three weeks since Paris, and I was now sleeping at night even though I was beyond a broken heart, I tried to keep a positive attitude. And even though I did manage to keep Lucas out of my head, I couldn't keep him out of my heart. In the beginning he called many times, but when I had refused to speak to him, the calls stopped.

"Ellen, Mary is asking you to speak to you." Edward said. I went to her room, wondering why she wanted to talk to me. Hi, how are feeling? I spend many hours with her and I knew her health was declining. "Ellen, I was thinking that you

need to take some time off and go visit your family." "No Mary, I want to stay with you." "I have already made arrangements for a car I want you to get some perspective on your life, take a few days and visit with your sister, you have been through so much with Lucas and the trip to Paris and the disappointment, I feel like it will do you good to get away,"

"Are you sure?" "Yes dear, just step away from everything for a while, let your hair down, enjoy some time with your family, I have seen you in here every day watching over me, you shouldn't be copped up in here watching an old lady sleep, you should be enjoying your life," "But I'm in here because I want to help take care of you." "Child, I have so many people trying to take care of me, but only the good lord can take care of me, Go have a nice visit." I gave her a hug goodbye then I went

and packed a few things and left, it did feel good to be driving again toward my hometown, it would be a big surprise for my sister to see me come for a visit. The hometown looked the same; it brought a fresh wave of tears as I remembered Matt and Tara.

Mary was right I did need to get away from everything, it was so good to see Sara and Kendal and Jason. After I told Sara I had called off the wedding, she didn't pressure me into talking about it and I was glad. I took them out to dinner and then to a movie, I laughed and for just a little while I forgot about Lucas and what might have been.

Sara told me she was so much happier being divorced, she no longer had to support him or answer to him, she looked so much better, she looked happy which she hadn't wear that emotion in years, I had a feeling she wasn't telling me the whole story because I had a hunch she may be seeing someone.

The next day I had lunch with Patty and Angie. It felt like old times when we were in high school, they tried to ask me questions about Paris, but I kept changing the subject, they finally got the hint that I did not want to talk about it. They both were married with children, I envied them, they seem so happy.

I stayed a few nights then decided to go back to Mary's. This visit did help me, I didn't see Dad, and I did try to call but only got his voicemail.

Chapter Thirty

Edward met me at the front door. "Ellen I have some bad news." "What? what's wrong Edward?" I already knew the news wasn't good. "It's Mrs. Ramsey; she passed away last night in her sleep. "No" I cried... "I knew I shouldn't have left, but she insisted." "No Ellen, Mary knew she was dying and that is why she sent you away, she told me that you had been through so much that she didn't want you to see her die."

"I'm so sorry"   I ran to my room and cried, I couldn't believe everything that was happening to me, it was like I was getting kicked when I was down. What was I going to do now? I wasn't waiting around to find out what was going to happen, because I knew James would be coming to Mary's funeral and I wasn't going to be here. I couldn't take anymore grief or disappointment.

The next morning I left to go find an apartment I could start new, with what savings I had, it would keep me until I could get a job. I was heartbroken that I couldn't attend Mary's service, but I couldn't take a change of seeing James or possibly Lucas. At the end of the day with no luck finding anything I had no other choice but to go back to my same apartment building and hope there was a vacancy. She had one on the lower floor which was slightly better than my old apartment, so I took it. On my way back to Mary's I kept telling myself this was only temporary.

Edward kept insisting on me staying until matter were taken care of , but I told him I couldn't and I asked if he could please make arrangements for my things to be taken to my new place. As I was packing my things, I didn't see a need to take the lovely gowns, so I just left them hanging in the closet. I didn't get much sleep that night, I cried for Mary and for Lucas and for myself.

It was sad to be back to where I started from; I knew a job would help me take my mind off of things. So Once again I searched the want ads. When I found nothing, I walked up town to put my application in some places that were close to my apartment since I didn't have a car, I couldn't afford to be choosy
It seemed like everywhere I went was a dead end.

I was so depressed I laid on the couch and cried, I had been looking for a job for three weeks and finding nothing, I knew my money was getting very low, I didn't know what I was going to do, I tried calling my Dad for a loan but he didn't return my calls. I felt so alone and I didn't know what to do. I started to think about my life growing up and I wondered how it went from a great childhood to this? How did I get myself in this condition, what could I have did differently in my life. My Dad wasn't even claiming to be my father anymore, and I knew it was because of Pat, what kind of hold could a woman have on a man to make him disown his children?

I have been wondering about my read mother, what she was like, was she remarried, Lucas only said she lived in Italy, I wish now I would have asked him more questions. I also wondered if she was sorry she gave me up?

Chapter Thirty One

The next day was Saturday, I would have to wait until Monday and start again on job hunting, I just laid around all day. There was nothing I wanted to do; I guess I fell into a self-pity mold. That afternoon, I was warming a can of soup, when someone knocked on my door, thinking it was just my landlady wanting her rent money, I answered it in my bathrobe.

There stood Lucas. "Lucas what are you doing here?" I was shocked and embarrassed not only for the way I looked but because of leaving without telling him why and because of my shabby apartment. There were a lot of reasons to be embarrassed right now. "I came because I think you owe me something!" "Lucas, I'm sorry, I know you are upset with me and you have every right to be,"   "Upset with you? yes I'm really upset with you, you left and didn't have the decency to even tell me why, I go to your hotel only to find a small package with the ring in it at the front desk, what was I supposed to think? He sounded so angry. "I sent you a message." I said. "Yes a message that read, I'm sorry Lucas but I have changed my mind about marrying you, was that an explanation to me Ellen?"

"No of course not, I'm sorry Lucas I didn't want to tell you." "Tell me what?" I could tell he was getting frustrated with me. "Lucas, I'm your sister, and I found this out when I saw the photos of your mother that day in the liberty." The tears were falling down my face. "What are you talking about? Now he just looked annoyed. "I will be right back" I went into the bedroom to get the photos of Riley. "As I handed him the pictures, I told him that Victoria was also my mother. "Victoria is your Mother?" He looked up at me with a very confused look on his face.

"Yes, can't you see why I couldn't tell you, I was so confused I just ran, I know I did things the wrong way, I know now I should have told you, and I'm sorry." "Yes, you should have told me, because

then I could have told you that Victoria is my step mother, my father married her when I was five years old." "But you said she was your mother?" "Because that is what I have always called her, I was five years old when she came into my life." "I also told you my Mom lived in Italy; I guess I should have been more précised about my mothers." "I didn't know what to say, I didn't know where this left us, had I blown my chance with Lucas by running and not talking to him? Did he still love me or want to be with me? I had to wait and let him make that choice. But my heart cried that it would be a choice in my favor because I loved him so much. It felt so great when he puts his arms around and he began to cry. "Ellen, you don't know what I have been through these last months, you had me so worried, I didn't even realize how much I loved you until you were gone." Then he got down on his knee again. "Ellen, I know I have asked you before, but I guess we should have gotten all the ghost out of the closet first and talked more, I love you and I still want to spent the rest of my life with you, if you will still have me since we were almost related.," he laughed, and I was pretty sure he was laughing at me, but I didn't care because once again my heart had found joy. "I love you so much" I cried and that was all I was able to get out of my mouth because of the tears. He placed my beautiful ring back on my finger... "This is never to come off again!" he sternly said. "Never" I said.

As I put my arms around his neck. "How did you find me? "Edward told me where you moved, I'm so sorry about Mary, she was a kind lady, and I will forever be thankful to her for bringing you to me

Chapter Thirty Two

Our wedding ceremony took place in the Rodin Garden, my gown was designed by Laure de sagazan. If I had my diary from when I was a child, today I would write these words....... It happened I got the wedding of my dreams.

Our honeymoon was surreal, we traveled to Bora Bora Island, and stayed at the Bora Bora resort, I had never seen anything like it not even in magazines

Our resort has private plunge pools overlooking Mount Otemanu, it even had glass flooring, and it was so beautiful. There was a colorful sea life beneath the floor. The view of the majestic mountain was breathtaking to say the least. Our bungalow was right on the water, it was a paradise, with great hospitality. We had so much fun and it was good just to relax and forget our cares, which right now, I didn't have a care in the world, I was truly blessed beyond words. We laid in the sun and we talked about our lives, about our families, by the time we got home, we knew everything about each other.

Chapter Thirty Three

The more I looked at my mother’s portrait, the more questions I had, so I decided to talk to James about her, I was sure Lucas had told him about me being her daughter. James, would you mind telling me about Victoria?”

“ I was wondering when this day would come that you would want to know about your mother.” “

What would you like to know?" " Did she ever talk about me?" " Oh yes, many times., when she started to regain her memory, she told me about having a daughter, she told me that her older sister took you and raised you as her own, she said she never got the opportunity to see you, and she had always wondered what you looked like and how you were doing." She chose not to see me when I was born, and why didn't she try to see me, or to contact her sister, my mother worried about her and thought she was dead, why was she so selfish."   " Honey, I don't have the answers that you are looking for, I think you should go and talk to Victoria yourself and ask her these questions,   I think it would do both of you a lot of good."

" I can't go see her I don't even know her, and besides I'm not sure I ever want to see her or talk

with her, I didn't leave her, she left me."

" I can understand that." James was very sympathetic toward me and I appreciate that since I knew he still loved her.

Lucas and I settled down in our married life, occasionally we would dress up and go to a dinner party, but we both liked to just go bike riding or have a picnic in the park, or go down and sat and watch the boats and many times we would visit the Eiffel tower, it became my favorite place. After a year we started talking about a family, I was more than ready. And it didn't take me long to get pregnant, we were very happy, especially James, he told me he didn't think he would ever be a grandfather. During my pregnancy I often thought of Tara, my sweet angel that was nested in the arms of god. I prayed for God to give us a son, and he did, a beautiful baby boy that looked just like his very proud daddy, how could Good bless me more?

We named him Bryson James, after his grandpa. When Bryson was eight months old, I had just put him down for his nap, when Lucas asked me to come into the liberty. I walked in and seen Victoria or Riley sitting on the long leather sofa looking more beautiful than she had a right too. "Hi Ellen, even her voice was nice." "Hello" "Please sit Ellen, James motioned for me to sit down. "I bought Victoria here today because I believe you two need to talk, I know Ellen you have questions you want to ask Victoria, and I know she also wants to ask you some questions, so we are going to leave you alone so you can talk." They walked out of the room. "Ellen first I just want to tell you how sorry I am, for not getting in touch with you, but I was so ashamed of my life back than and the things that I did, I just couldn't face you or my sister. "Why did you give me up?"

"I was sixteen and I was scared." Scared of what, that I would upset your life? ruin your plans?" " No, I just got in over my head with something and the only thing I knew to do was to run." " You ran and you never looked back, you didn't care about me." " No Ellen, you are wrong, I did care about you and I grieved for you."

" How do you expect me to believe that when you never tried to contact me, and what about your own sister that raised and loved you, my dad told me she used to cry every night about you, not knowing if you were alive or dead, and she went to her grave thinking you were dead".

"Ellen, it's more complicated than that, you wouldn't understand." "Oh I think I do understand, a baby would just have complicated

your carefree life, so you took the easy way out, and dumped your problem on the one person that loved you more than anyone, you knew she would do anything for you and that included raising your child, and just so you know. I'm thankful you gave me the best mom in the world, she was a saint, and I loved her." *" I know she was and I loved her too, one of the reasons I stayed away, because I didn't want to hurt her." She started to cry. But I knew her tears were as fake as her eyelashes and I wasn't buying them.*

Chapter Thirty Four

Who is my Father?" I asked... She looked at me confused. ""What do you mean who is your father?" " Well no one seemed to know, so I was hoping at least you would know." " Ellen, what did your parents tell you?' "My mother told me you were young and you had run off with a man and when you came back you were pregnant with me and you were going to put me up for adoption and they took me, and that you left and no one heard from you again."

I will admit when I was young, I was very unsettled and I wanted more out of life than what my sister wanted, I didn't want to have a family and live the boring life, I seen my sister living, but I want fun and adventure, I wanted to see the world."

" Then why were you so careless to get pregnant?"

" Well because I was careless, but for not the reason you think."

"You didn't answer my question, who is my father?" She looked at me for a long time before she spoke. My sister is gone now, so I guess you

can know the truth, your father is the same man that you have always known as your father." " What?" Yes he really is your father, and as far as I know your mother never knew, thank goodness." " You want to tell me what you are talking about please." I was starting to get very upset on what I think she was telling me. "Ellen, I was just a girl, but he should have known better than to take advantage of a child, he was a man with a wife and a child. It happened one night when I came home late from hanging out with friends, I was trying to unlock the front door when I heard him say my name, I turned and he was standing at the corner of the house. "Come here I need to show you something." I wasn't scared because I never thought I had a reason to be scared, but I should have been, he raped me that night and then he begged me not to tell my sister, *he kept apologizing and saying he would never touch me again and how much it would hurt my sister if she knew. After that night I couldn't stand to look at him, and I was too a shame to look my sister in the dace, even though it wasn't my fault, I was just a girl."*

" So is that why you left?"

"There was a truck driver that I knew and he was always trying to get me to go places with him, so I packed my clothes and I left. My life got bad real fast, I was dumped when I wouldn't sleep with him, I had no place to go, and then I found out I was pregnant with you, so I decided to go home and tell your Dad that he would have to give me money for the baby, but he told me he would take the baby and they would raise you and give you a good home. He gave me one thousand dollars to go away, but I never forgot you, but I knew you

were better off with them, they could give you what I couldn't."

"Oh my goodness, if what you just told me is true, then that makes my father a jerk, after they told me I wasn't there daughter he has acted so innocent, knowing all the time this was his fault."

"Ellen, I think you should have a talk with him."

Chapter Thirty Five

After I told Lucas everything, he insisted he go with me to visit my father.

I wanted to know the truth before I told Sara but if what she told me was true, Sara would know before I come to back to Paris.

She was so happy to see us and to meet Bryson; he took to her right away. "Sara have you heard from Dad?' " He calls now and then, he took me and the kids to dinner last month, I think he is starting to see how Pat really is," "Why doesn't he answer my phone calls?" "I don't know," "Well tomorrow, he will have to talk to me because I'm going to his house." "I know he will be glad to see you." "We will see." "Hey ladies, Bryson, and I are ready to go to the restaurant." Lucas said. We had a very pleasant evening with my sister and her now teenagers, plus I got to meet her fiancé and I really liked him. The next morning I called Dad's cell first I only got his voicemail; I called his home phone also to get an answering machine... I had asked Lucas to please stay with Bryson so I could speak to my father alone. I drove to his work only to be told that this was his day off. My next stop was his house. I knocked and Pat came to the door, looking very disappointed when she seen me standing on her porch. "Hey Pat, how are you?" "I'm fine, I'm not sure your Father is up yet I will have to check," She started to close the door without inviting me in but I put my foot in to stop the door from closing, she just gave a strange look and took a deep breath like she was about to say something but changed her mind. Only seconds later Dad came to the door, obviously he had been out of bed for hours. "Ellen how are you, what a nice surprise, come in." "No Dad, can we talk outside please?" I wasn't about to go into that woman's house and let her give me dirty looks. "Yes let's sit on the porch." He pointed to one of the chairs, after we were seated, even though I went over this conversation a million times in my head, I didn't know what to say.

"Ellen, how is Paris? I would love to meet the man that made all of your dreams come true, and my new grandson, Bryson, isn't it?" " Dad, what I need to talk to you about is very hard for me, I don't even know where to start."

" It sounds serious whatever it is."

" I found Riley, she did not drown" "That woman let my poor wife believe she was dead, she is selfish and I hope I never see her again, I wish she would have drown for what she did." He sounded so hateful and mean. "What about what you did, Dad?" I saw his face start to turn white. "What are you talking about?" his voce rose. "Are you my real Dad?" "Ellen I told you I would always be your Dad, didn't I?" "I didn't come all this way to play word games with you, did you rape Riley, and are you my real father, yes or no? Just give me a true answer."

"I don't know what that woman has been telling you?" "Okay, will you have a DNA test please for me?' " Ellen, when you want to come here and visit with me that will be fine, but no I won't have a test done." He got up and walked in the house and for the first time I actually hoped he wasn't my father. Because this was not the man that loved me and raised me, to me he was nothing more than a stranger. That evening we took Kendal and Jason to our hotel to swim in the pool, I knew Lucas wasn't accustomed to this kind of hotels but this was the nicest one in this town. I was sitting on the edge of the pool with Bryson when my Dad called me. "Ellen can you meet me at the park in an hour? "Yes I will be there."

Chapter Thirty Six

I Had been waiting for over an hour and I thought he had changed his mind, just as I was about to leave, he pulled up. He walked up and I could tell that what Riley had told me was the truth even before my Dad spoke a word. We just looked at each other. "It's true, isn't it Dad?" "Yes what she told you was all true and I'm very sorry I did it," "Did Mom know?" "No it would have killed her." "Were you just going to keep pretending like you didn't know who my real father was?" "I thought it was better this way." "Better for whom? Dad"

"Ellen, I'm trying to ask you to forgive me and please let's just keep this secret buried please, I'm your father and I have always been your father from day one." "I do forgive you, but it's not me you should be asking forgiveness from." "I will never speak or see that woman again, and I'm telling as your father to please don't let her into your life..." "Sorry Dad this time the choice is not yours."

I didn't tell Sara like I had planned to do;

I decided to just let it go.

Once we got back home, I told Victoria I wanted to get to know her if she wanted it too. "Oh Ellen, I do this makes me so happy."

This time I knew her tears were real.

Chapter Thirty Seven

Victoria spend a lot of time at our house getting to know me and Bryson, and I loved having her there, and also I knew James loved having her there.

And it wasn't long before a small elegant ceremony with just family and close friends took place. I was thrilled because now I could call her mom without the confusion.

"Ellen I was thinking we could get the grandparents to watch Bryson and we could go on a little cruise just the two of us,"

"Lucas that sound so awesome, ask me again in about six months." "Are you serious?" "Yes, I found out this morning, are you happy?" "I'm very happy, and I know Bryson will be very happy to be having a brother or sister,"

"Let's keep it a secret for just a little while, Okay?" "Okay, I will try." He was all smiles, I knew before the day was over everyone would know, my husband could not keep a secret.

Don came to visit me with his new wife, it was so good to see my older brother, and He loved Paris, and promised he would be back.

Don and Lucas became fast friends, his wife was very beautiful and sweet, and I could tell my brother was very happy.

I know that God takes what is broken and he puts it back together, my heart was so full when I held my baby daughter. "Now our family is compete, a son and now a daughter, I am a blessed man." Lucas said as he kissed me.

Once again I thought on Dr. Adams's words "Ellen, It is normal to cry and be depressed, but you need to keep putting one foot in front of the other, just be Patient With yourself, you will not always feel the way you feel right now. There is no schedule time for when you should feel certain emotions, but one day, you will smile again."

James had made the statement one time that the portrait of Victoria would never be took down but today it was moved to a different wall and in its place was a large portrait with James & Victoria, Me & Lucas, Bryson and his baby Sister Emma. And in my hand I held a photo of Tara.... Lest I forget.

Made in the USA
Monee, IL
30 August 2020